Desmond
1
Dinosaur

Desmond is Lonely

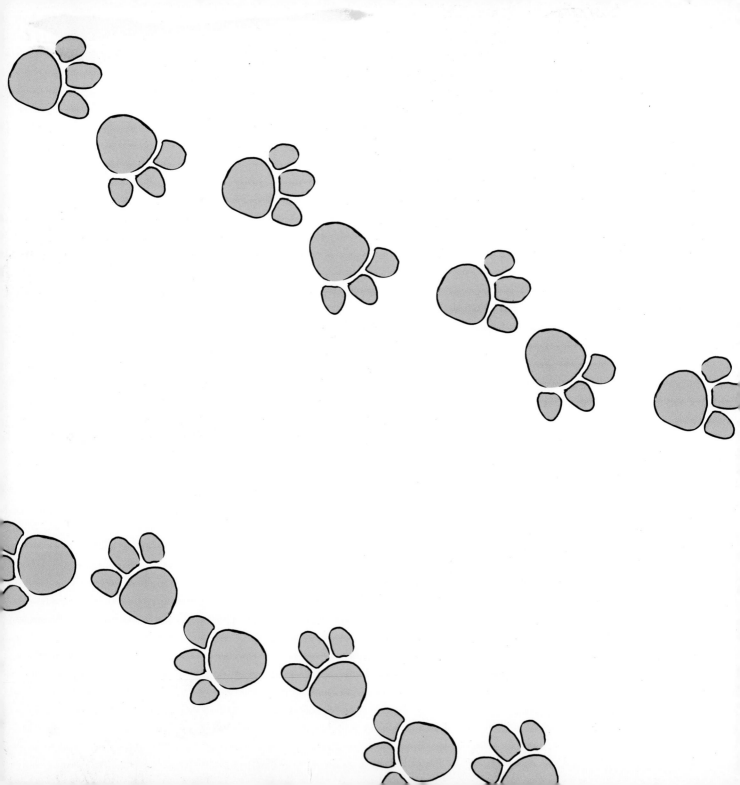

This book
belongs to

_____

In memory of George Harding,
a generous and kind friend.

Desmond the Dinosaur Series

Desmond is Lonely
Desmond Starts School
Desmond Goes to the Vet
Desmond and the Monsters

HAPPY CAT BOOKS

Published by Happy Cat Books Ltd.
Bradfield, Essex CO11 2UT, UK

This edition published 2003
1 3 5 7 9 10 8 6 4 2

A CIP catalogue record for this book is available from the British Library

ISBN 1 903285 50 X Paperback

Printed in Poland, DRUK INTRO SA

Desmond
1
Dinosaur

Desmond is Lonely

Althea

Illustrated by Sarah Wimperis

Happy Cat Books

Desmond was a very miserable and lonely dinosaur.

He was living many millions of years after
his proper time, and he didn't think he had
any friends.

People stared and pointed at him when he walked down the street.

Being a shy sort of dinosaur, Desmond hated being stared at and so he always hurried on.

One day Desmond
went to the market
to do his shopping.
He was rather fussy
about his food, but
he was very fond of
lettuces and oranges.

He always went to the same stall because George, the fruit and veg man was kind and did not stare.
He always treated Desmond with respect.

"Hello, Mr Desmond, Sir, what can we do for you today?" said George.
"I have some nice juicy oranges from Spain,"

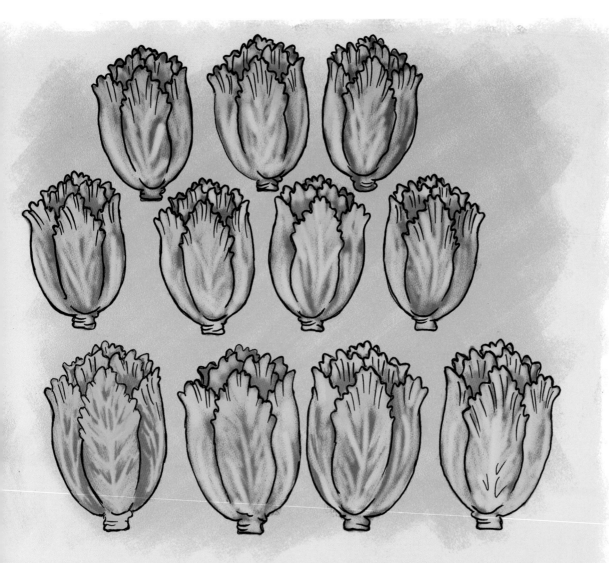

"- And I think you will find these lettuces tasty.
Perhaps you would like a couple?"
"- or maybe a dozen?" he added.

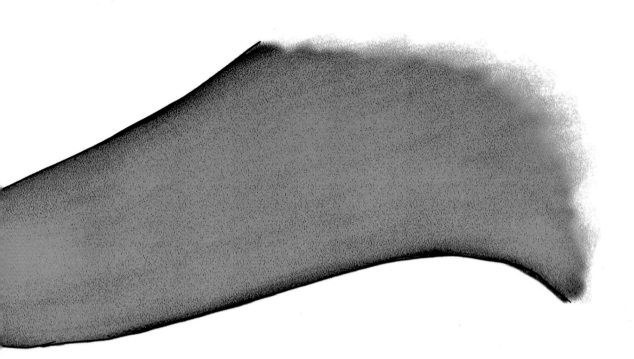

Desmond said that he would take the dozen as he was particularly hungry.
(He was really rather big, and although he hated to admit it, he was also a bit greedy!)

Just then a lady came up to the stall and asked for a lettuce.

"Oh dear," said George, "I have just sold the last dozen. Would you like some carrots instead?"

"No thank you. I'm sorry, but carrots won't do at all. I want a lettuce to make sandwiches for my garden party," explained the lady.

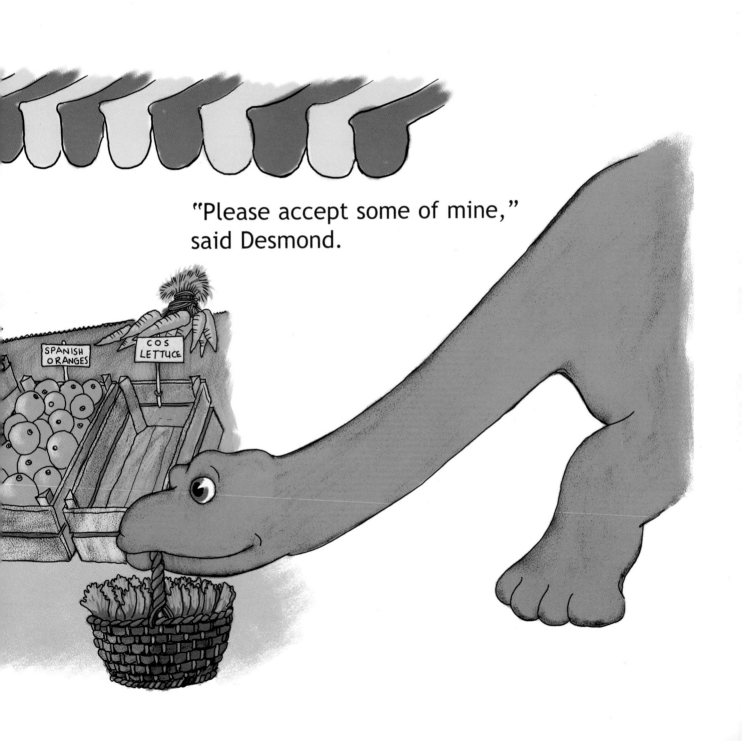

"Please accept some of mine," said Desmond.

"That is most kind of you," exclaimed the lady.
"Would you like to come to my garden party?"

"Ooh, yes please! I should love to come," said Desmond.

"Come along to my house then," said the lady.

They said goodbye to George and set off. Desmond was very excited.

At the party the lady introduced Desmond to all her friends, and told them how kind he had been.

Everyone agreed that Desmond was quite the nicest dinosaur they had ever met.

For ever afterwards,
when Desmond went out
walking or shopping
people waved and
called, "Hello Desmond!"

Desmond was very happy. He didn't think he would ever be shy or lonely again.

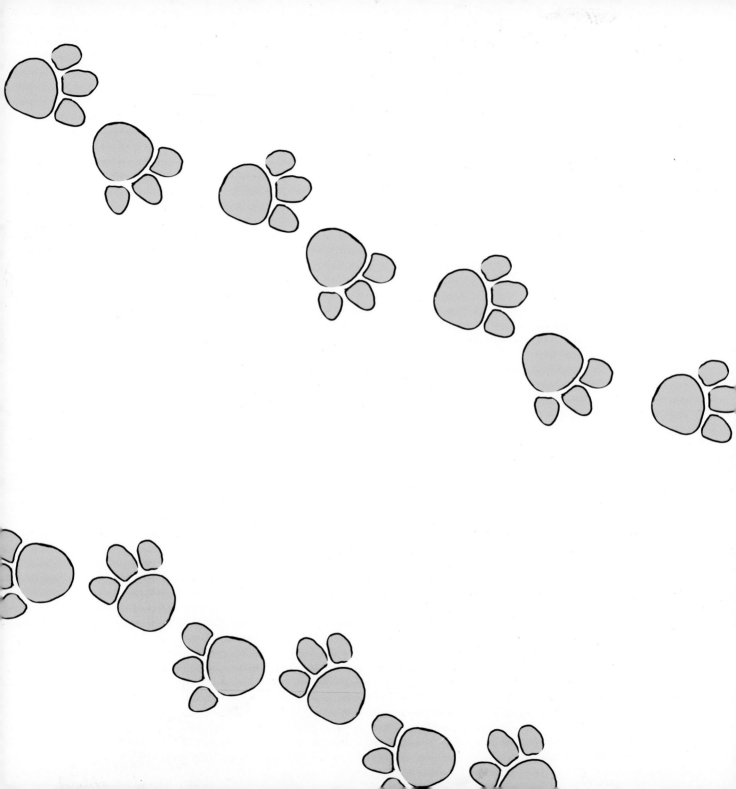

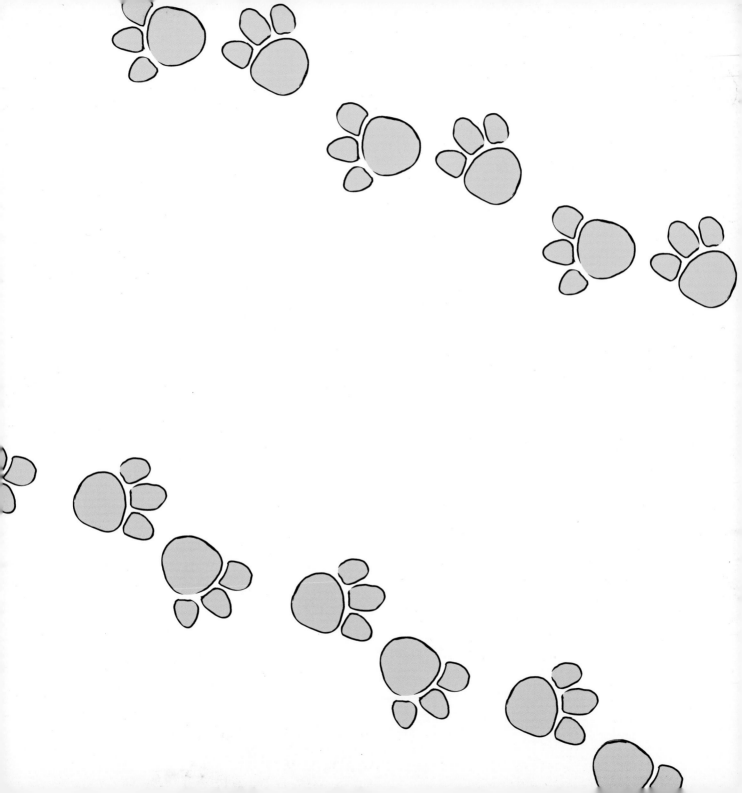